If your child struggles with a word, you can encourage "sounding it out," but keep in mind that not all words can be sounded out. Your child might pick up clues about a word from the picture, other words in the sentence, or any rhyming patterns. If your child struggles with a word for more than five seconds, it is usually best to simply say the word.

Most of all, remember to praise your child's efforts and keep the reading fun. After you have finished the book, ask a few questions and discuss what you have read together. Rereading this book multiple times may also be helpful for your child.

Try to keep the tips above in mind as you read together, but don't worry about doing everything right. Simply sharing the enjoyment of reading together will increase your child's reading skills and help to start your child off on a lifetime of reading enjoyment!

We Both Read: My Town

Published by Treasure Bay, Inc.
P.O. Box 119
Novato, CA 94948 USA

Printed in Singapore

Library of Congress Catalog Card Number: 2006907939

Hardcover ISBN-13: 978-1-60115-001-1
Paperback ISBN-13: 978-1-60115-002-8

We Both Read® Books
Patent No. 5,957,693

Visit us online at:
www.webothread.com

PR 07/11

WE BOTH READ®

My Town

By Sindy McKay

Illustrated by Meredith Johnson

TREASURE BAY

My dad and I like to go driving around.

He wants me to know where things are in my . . .

. . . town.

We're drawing a map of my town that's so neat!

It shows where my house is. It shows my whole . . .

. . . street.

I live near the corner of Third Street and Drew.

My address is one hundred seventy . . .

. . . two.

Now just up the street lives my best friend, Dan Coop.

I mark where he lives with a basketball . . .

. . . hoop.

We go to a school that's near Second and Hop.

The sign on the corner is red and reads . . .

. . . STOP.

Turn *right* at the sign then the street takes a jag.

The school is right there. You can see a big . . .

. . . flag.

Now if you turn *left* at the corner instead, you'll come to the market where you can buy . . .

. . . bread.

Our map tells me where the police stations are.
I've marked every one with a gold colored . . .

. . . star.

The firehouse sits up on Sycamore Street.
I sat in the truck once, right in the front . . .

. . . seat.

The hospital sits on a hill by a farm.

It's where my dad took me when I broke . . .

. . . my arm.

Now finding the library isn't that hard.
I walk there with Mom, but I use my own . . .

. . . card.

My dad and I work on this map as a team.

The blue color means there's a river or . . .

. . . stream.

⌾ Our map shows the west and the east side of town.

The north side **is** up and the south side . . .

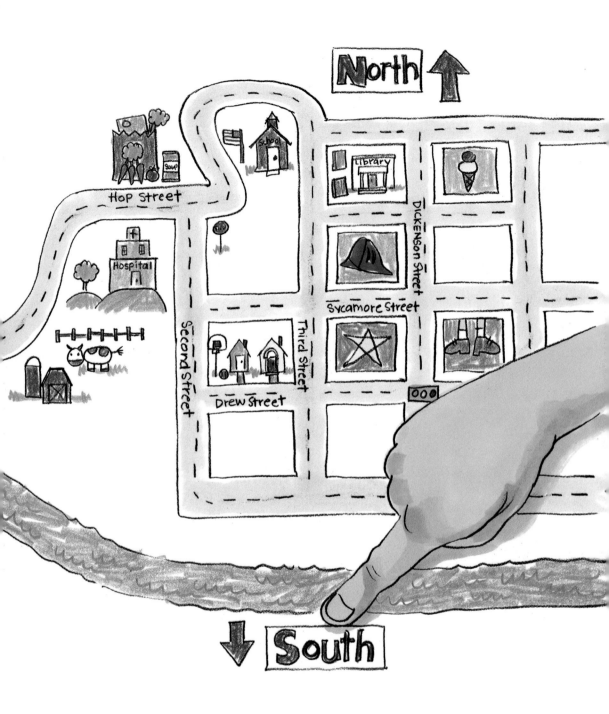

... **is** down.

My dad says we're going to "Stickles
and Stones."
They have just the biggest and best . . .

. . . ice cream cones.

We walk out the door and I put on my cap.

To help find the way I have made a small . . .

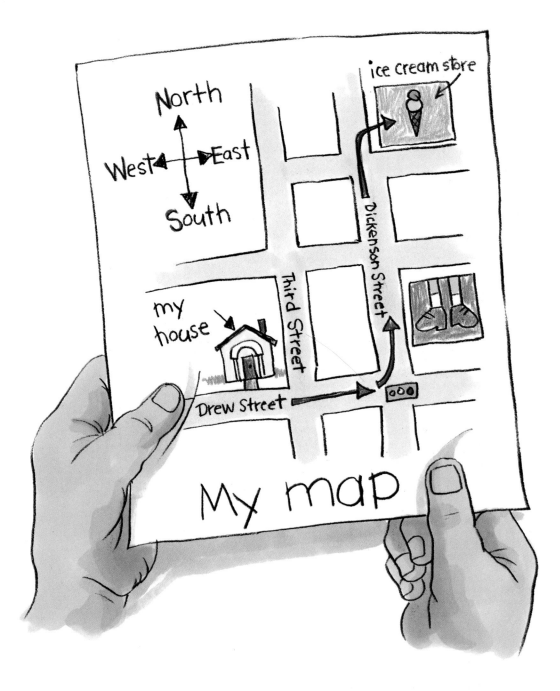

. . . map.

On Drew, we head east going straight to the light.

From there, do we turn to the left or . . .

. . . the right?

We'll turn to the left onto Dickenson Street.

Go north past the shoe store. I marked that with . . .

. . . feet.

We count two blocks more then we finally stop.

I'm ordering chocolate with sprinkles on . . .

. . . top.

To find any place in my town is a snap!

We just plan **our** route there by using . . .

. . . **our** map!

The End

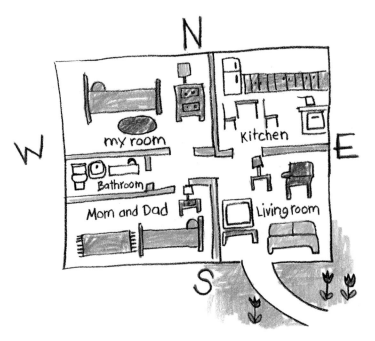

In this story, a boy and his father have a great time working together to draw a map of all the important places in their town. You can have fun drawing maps too! Here are some ideas to help you get started.

Start by first drawing a map of your house. Once you are familiar with the way a map works, you can try making a map of your neighborhood. Be sure you include your own address and the names of the streets that are around you. You can also make a map that shows how to get to a place near your house that you like to go to.

The boy in this story used a cone to show where his favorite ice cream shop is located and a basketball hoop to show where his best friend lives. You can make up your own symbols for the places that are special to you.

SOME OTHER FUN MAP ACTIVITIES

Ask an adult to make a treasure map and see if you can follow the directions to the treasure. You can even make your own treasure map!

The next time your family takes a trip, help your mom or dad map out the route you will take to your destination.

If you have access to a computer, your parents or teacher might be able to help you use the Internet to go to a site, such as Mapquest (www.mapquest.com), where you can create a map with directions from your house to a favorite location.

If you liked *My Town*, here are two other
We Both Read® Books you are sure to enjoy!

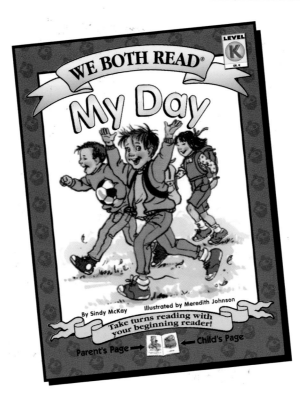

This Level K book is designed for the child who is
just being introduced to reading. The child's pages
have only one or two words, which relate directly to
the illustration and even rhyme with what has just
been read to them. This title is a charming story
about what a child does in the course of a simple
happy day.